HarperFestival is an imprint of HarperCollins Publishers.

The Angry Birds Movie: Laughtastic Joke Book
© 2016 Rovio Animation Ltd., Angry Birds, and all related properties, titles, logos, and
characters are trademarks of Rovio Entertainment Ltd. and Rovio Animation Ltd. and are
used with permission.
Library of Congress Control Number: 2015959754
ISBN 978-0-06-246407-1

16 17 18 19 20 PC/RRDH 10 9 8 7 6 5 4 3 2 1
❖
First Edition

THE ANGRY BIRDS™ MOVIE

LAUGHTASTIC JOKE BOOK

BY COURTNEY CARBONE

HARPER FESTIVAL

An Imprint of HarperCollinsPublishers

Contents

WELCOME TO BIRD ISLAND

Welcome to Bird Island, where the sun shines brightly, the breezes are gentle, and the birds are a happy, cheerful, funny bunch. Even those few birds who are prone to angry outbursts love a good laugh. They've collected some of their favorite jokes and riddles for you here in this book. And as an extra-special surprise, Bird Island's newest inhabitants—the pigs—are sharing their favorite one-liners and puns, too.

SO GET READY TO GET SILLY.

Meet the Flock

Red
Angriest Bird on the Island

Chuck
Red's Fast Friend

TERENCE
The Gentle Giant

BOMB
Most Explosive Personality

MATILDA
Positively Positive

STELLA
ISLAND ENTHUSIAST

SHIRLEY
OLDEST BIRD ON THE ISLAND

MIGHTY EAGLE
BIRD ISLAND HERO

JUDGE PECKINPAH
BIRD ISLAND AUTHORITY

CYRUS
THE JUDGE'S LITTLE "HELPER"

EDWARD, EVA, AND TIMOTHY
A BIRD-FECT FAMILY

MEET THE PIGS

LEONARD
PIG MAN ON CAMPUS

ROSS
ASSISTANT PIG MAN

PIGGIES
100%
RIDICULOUS

RUN, RED, RUN

Being punctual is no laughing matter, especially when you have to be on time for a surprise bird-day party. But when you're Red and the only thing standing between you and making it to a bird-day party on time is a vine-filled, booby-trapped jungle, a sense of humor definitely helps!

WHY DID RED GET LOST CHASING AFTER THE EGG?

IT WAS A JUNGLE IN THERE!

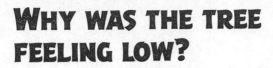

WHY WAS THE TREE FEELING LOW?

IT WAS STUMPED!

WHY WAS RED RUNNING AROUND IN CIRCLES?

IT WAS EASIER THAN RUNNING AROUND IN SQUARES!

WHAT DID THE FLOWER DO WHEN IT GOT LOST?

IT FOUND A NEW ROOT!

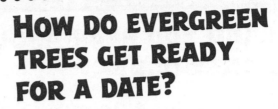

HOW DO EVERGREEN TREES GET READY FOR A DATE?

THEY SPRUCE THEMSELVES UP!

WHAT DO MAPLE TREES DOWNLOAD ONTO THEIR SMART PHONES?

S'APPS

WHY ARE PINE TREES GOOD AT SEWING?

THEY ALWAYS CARRY NEEDLES!

DID YOU HEAR ABOUT THE SILLY OAK?

IT LOVED TO TELL ACORN-Y JOKES!

HOW DID THE TREE STAY WARM IN WINTER?

IT WORE A FIR COAT!

WHAT DID THE FALLEN TREE ASK?

"WOOD YOU GIVE ME A HAND?"

WHAT DID THE SHRUB'S VOICE MAIL SAY?

"PLEASE LEAF A MESSAGE!"

WHAT DO YOU CALL A YOUNG TREE'S ALLOWANCE?

SEED MONEY

WHAT IS A TREE'S FAVORITE SNACK?

PEPPERMINT BARK

19

WHERE DO BABY
TREES GROW UP?

IN A NURSERY

20

WHAT STORY DO LITTLE SPROUTS LISTEN TO AT BEDTIME?

"THE TREE LITTLE TWIGS"

HOW DID THE TREE BREAK THE LAW?

IT COMMITTED TREE-SON!

HOW DO TREES SHOW THAT THEY CARE?

THEY GO OUT ON A LIMB!

WHY DID THE TREE HANG OUT WITH LIFEGUARDS?

IT WAS A BEECH!

WHY DID THE TREE MAKE NEW FRIENDS?

SHE WANTED TO BRANCH OUT.

FOLKS, HOW WOULD YOU DESCRIBE LIFE ON BIRD ISLAND?

It's My Party and I'll Joke if I Want To

Whether it's a hatchling's first bird-day party or another big blowout for Shirley, Bird Island puts on the silliest events. The key ingredient to throwing a perfect party: laughter.

FORGET ABOUT THE PAST; YOU CAN'T CHANGE IT.

FORGET ABOUT THE FUTURE; YOU CAN'T PREDICT IT.

FORGET ABOUT THE PRESENT; THAT'S WHAT BOMB DID.

HE FORGOT TO GET YOU A PRESENT.

WHY DID RED TAKE THE CAKE DELIVERY JOB?

IT WAS A SWEET DEAL!

HOW DID RED PLAN HIS ROUTE?

HE WAS WINGING IT!

WHAT DID EDWARD THINK OF RED'S EXCUSE?

HE DIDN'T GIVE A HOOT!

WHY DID BOMB BRING A GOLF CLUB TO THE BIRD-DAY PARTY?

HE WANTED TO HELP PUTT THE CAKE!

WHAT'S RED'S LEAST FAVORITE PARTY GAME?

PIN THE TAIL ON THE ANGRY BIRD

WHAT DO BIRDS SING ON THEIR BIRD-DAYS?

"HATCHY BIRD-DAY TO YOU"

WHAT DO YOU GET WHEN YOU HIT YOUR BIRD-DAY CAKE WITH A HAMMER?

A POUND CAKE

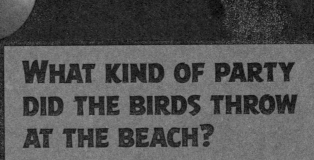

WHAT KIND OF PARTY DID THE BIRDS THROW AT THE BEACH?

A SHELL-ABRATION

WHAT GOES UP BUT NEVER COMES DOWN?

YOUR AGE

WHAT DID THE FROSTING SAY TO THE CAKE?

"I'M STUCK ON YOU!"

WHAT DID THE CANDLE ASK THE CAKE?

"WHAT'S EATING YOU?"

WHY WAS THE CANDLE SO MAD?

BIRD-DAYS REALLY BURNED IT UP!

WHY WASN'T ANYONE EATING THE MARBLE CAKE?

IT HURT THEIR TEETH!

WHAT DO YOU ALWAYS GET ON YOUR BIRD-DAY?

ANOTHER YEAR OLDER

WHY DID TIMOTHY YELL AT HIS CAKE?

IT WAS AN I-SCREAM CAKE!

WHY DID TERENCE MISS THE PARTY?

HE WAS A LITTLE UNDER THE FEATHER!

WHAT KIND OF BIRD-DAY CAKE DOES JUDGE PECKINPAH AVOID?

SHORTCAKE

WHY WAS THE CANDLE ALWAYS TIRED?

BECAUSE THERE'S NO REST FOR THE WICKED

LIGHTS, CAMERA, LAUGHTER

The rumors are true. Red had an unfortunate angry outburst at the Bird Island movie theater, but that's because he's a huge movie fan. All the birds on the island love going to the movies . . . especially the ones that make them laugh.

WHAT MAKES BIRD ISLAND A GREAT PLACE TO MAKE MOVIES?

IT HAS PLENTY OF EGG-STRAS!

WHY DID RED GO TO A SILENT MOVIE?

HE DIDN'T WANT ANYONE TALKING TO HIM, INCLUDING THE ACTORS!

WHAT'S CHUCK'S FAVORITE MOVIE?

THE FAST AND THE FURIOUS

Why did Bomb wear a cast to the movie set?

He was looking for his big break!

Did you hear about the actor who fell through the floor?

He was just going through a stage!

What do the best actors on Bird Island win?

Egg-cademy Awards

Which birds make the best acting partners?

Toucans

WHO BRINGS THE SOCCER PLAYERS DRINKS DURING HALF TIME?

THE WATERFOWL

WHICH BIRDS ARE THE MOST INTO SPORTS?

FANTAILS

WHICH BIRDS TALK THE MOST DURING MOVIES?

THE ONES ON THE SCREEN

WHAT DO YOU CALL A MOVIE ABOUT BOATS?

A DOCK-UMENTARY

WHY DID STELLA SEE THE MOVIE ALONE?

IT WAS AN INDEPENDENT FILM!

WHY DID THE ACTORS CARRY BAND-AIDS?

THE DIRECTOR KEPT YELLING "CUT!"

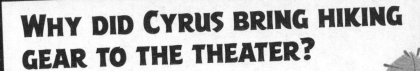

WHY DID CYRUS BRING HIKING GEAR TO THE THEATER?

HE HEARD THERE WAS A CLIFFHANGER!

WHAT KINDS OF MOVIES DO PIGS LIKE BEST?

ONES WITH A GREEN SCREEN

WHY WAS THE ACTOR FIRED?

HE WAS MAKING TOO BIG A SCENE!

WHY DID THE PIG BECOME AN ACTOR?

BECAUSE HE WAS A HAM

WHY DID THE AUDIENCE BRING COLD CUTS TO THE THEATER?

THEY HEARD THE MOVIE HAD SUBTITLES!

WHAT IS CHUCK'S FAVORITE PART OF A FILM?

WHEN THEY ZOOM IN

HOW DO THE CAST AND CREW TRAVEL AROUND?

BY MOVIE TRAILERS

WHY WAS THE BIRD SHARPENING HIS BEAK?

HE WAS AUDITIONING FOR A BIT PART!

WHY DID RED DROP HIS POPCORN?

HE HAD BUTTERFINGERS!

WHY DOES CHUCK ALWAYS TELL POPCORN JOKES?

BECAUSE HE'S CORNY

WHICH BIRDS ARE THE BEST ACTORS?

STARLINGS

WHY DIDN'T THE KERNEL LEAVE THE POPCORN TUB?

HE WAS CORN-FUSED!

43

TICKLING THE FUNNY BONES

Shirley always says:
A giggle a day keeps the doctor away . . .
unless it's time for your annual checkup . . .
or you're a little under the weather . . .
or you need a teeth cleaning.

WHY DID THE DOCTOR TAKE TERENCE'S TEMPERATURE?

HE WAS HOT-HEADED!

WHY WAS THE PATIENT LAUGHING?

THE DOCTOR HAD HIM IN STITCHES!

WHY DID THE DOCTOR QUIT HIS JOB?

HE DIDN'T HAVE ANY PATIENCE!

WHY DID BOMB BRING HIS PILLOW TO THE DOCTOR?

HE WAS FEELING ALL STUFFED UP!

WHY WAS BOMB AFRAID TO TAKE MEDICINE FOR A STOMACH ACHE?

HE DIDN'T HAVE THE GUTS!

WHY DID ALL THE BIRDS GO TO THE SAME SURGEON?

SHE WAS A CUT ABOVE THE REST!

WHY DID CHUCK BRING #2 PENCILS TO THE DOCTOR?

HE WAS THERE FOR AN EXAM!

WHY WAS RED'S TONGUE SO SAD?

THE DOCTOR HAD USED A DEPRESSOR!

WHY DID THE FORTUNE-TELLER SEE THE EYE DOCTOR?

HER VISION WAS GETTING CLOUDY!

WHAT DO DUCKS LIKE BEST ABOUT THE DOCTOR'S OFFICE?

THE WADING ROOM

WHY DID THE DOCTOR STUDY MEDICINE?

SHE THOUGHT SHE'D GIVE IT A SHOT!

WHY DIDN'T CHUCK LIKE HIS NEW DOCTOR?

HE THOUGHT HE WAS A QUACK!

WHEN IS TERENCE'S DENTIST APPOINTMENT?

TOOTH-HURTY

WHAT DO YOU GIVE A SICK BIRD?

TWEET-MENT

WHY DID THE COOKIE GO TO THE DOCTOR?

HE FELT A LITTLE CRUMBY.

WHY DID CYRUS GO TO THE DOCTOR WHEN HIS TAIL FEATHERS HURT?

HE WANTED TO GET TO THE BOTTOM OF IT.

HOW DOES THE DENTIST PRACTICE?

SHE DOES A LOT OF DRILLS.

WHAT DID JUDGE PECKINPAH SAY TO THE DENTIST?

"PULL MY TOOTH, THE WHOLE TOOTH, AND NOTHING BUT THE TOOTH."

WHY DID THE DOCTOR TAKE HIS TIME WITH THE ITCHY PATIENT?

HE DIDN'T WANT TO DO ANYTHING RASH.

WHY DID CHUCK SEE THE DOCTOR?

HE WAS WORRIED HE HAD YELLOW FEVER!

WHY DIDN'T SHIRLEY LIKE HER NEW FOOT DOCTOR?

HE WAS A REAL HEEL!

WHY DID THE HUSBAND AND WIFE GO TO THE DOCTOR TOGETHER?

THEY HAD JOINT PAIN.

WHY DID JUDGE PECKINPAH MAKE HIS WHOLE OFFICE GET A CHECKUP?

HE HEARD THERE WAS A STAFF INFECTION!

WHAT DOES IT MEAN WHEN BIRDS HAVE WRINKLY CLOTHES?

THEY HAVE AN IRON DEFICIENCY!

WHY DID TERENCE THINK HE WAS A BUMBLEBEE?

HE WAS COVERED IN HIVES!

WHY DID THE MAIL BIRD CALL OUT SICK?

SHE HAD POST-NASAL DRIP!

WHAT DO SINGLE BIRDS GET ON VALENTINE'S DAY?

HEARTBURN

WHY WERE THE BIRDS FEELING DOWN?

THEY WERE BLUEBIRDS!

WHY DID THE BIRD TRY TO BLOW A BUBBLE?

THE DENTIST SAID HE HAD GUM DISEASE!

WHY DID THE DOCTOR GIVE STELLA A BLANKET?

SHE HAD A COLD!

WHY DID EVERYONE AVOID THE BIRD VILLAGE PHARMACIST?

HE WAS A REAL PILL!

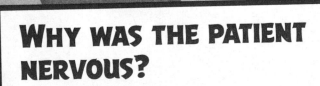

WHY WAS THE PATIENT NERVOUS?

HE HEARD THE DOCTOR WAS PRACTICING!

WHY DID THE BLOOD CELLS DROP OUT OF MEDICAL SCHOOL?

THE PRESSURE WAS TOO HIGH!

WHAT DID ONE BLOOD VIAL SAY TO THE OTHER?

"LOOK—YOU'RE MY TYPE!"

WHAT DID THE OTHER VIAL SAY BACK?

"ARE YOU POSITIVE?"

WHY DID THE LOSING TEAM GO TO THE HOSPITAL AFTER THEIR GAME?

THEY WERE SORE LOSERS!

FREE-RANGE FUN

The birds spend a lot of time outdoors—at the park, on the beach, playing on the soccer fields—and they always manage to have a lot of silly fun under the sun.

HOW DO BIRDS CHEER FOR THEIR SOCCER TEAMS?

THEY EGG THEM ON!

WHY DO SOCCER PLAYERS DO SO WELL IN SCHOOL?

THEY KNOW HOW TO USE THEIR HEADS!

WHAT TEA DO SOCCER PLAYERS DRINK?

PENAL-TEA

WHAT RUNS AROUND A SOCCER FIELD BUT NEVER MOVES?

A FENCE

WHY DID THE LITTLE BIRD PLAY SOCCER AGAINST RED'S HOUSE?

HE WAS HAVING A BALL!

WHY DID RED PUNT THE SOCCER BALL?

JUST FOR KICKS

WHY DOES RED AVOID PLAYING SOCCER?

HE ALWAYS GETS RED CARDS!

How easily did the mime find Red?

It was a walk in the park.

Where should the bird mime perform?

In a talon show

Why did the mime speak when out of character?

It was all an act!

What was Red doing in the park?

Bird-watching

WHAT KINDS OF BIRDS ARE ALWAYS FLIRTING?

LOVEBIRDS

HOW DID THE BIRDS' DATE GO?

PHEASANT-LY

WHICH BIRDS ARE THE MOST AFFECTIONATE?

KISS-ADEES

HOW DO BIRDS SAY "I LOVE YOU"?

WITH A PECK ON THE CHEEK

WHAT FISH IS MOST FAMOUS?

A STARFISH

WHY DOES TERENCE ALWAYS RIDE THE CAROUSEL?

HE LIKES TO MAKE THE ROUNDS!

WHAT DID THE BEACH SAY TO THE WAVE?

"LONG TIDE, NO SEA!"

WHAT DO YOU CALL WAVES ON SMALL BEACHES?

MICROWAVES

THE PUNS, THE WHOLE PUNS, AND NOTHING BUT THE PUNS

Judge Peckinpah presides over Bird Court and makes sure that justice prevails and the rules are followed by everyone on the island. But he doesn't object when the occasional joke is told in his court . . . especially when he's the one telling it!

WHY WAS RED SO ANGRY?

IT WAS A CROSS-EXAMINATION.

WHY WAS RED STUDYING BEFORE HIS TRIAL?

FOR HIS TEST-IMONY

WHY WAS JUDGE PECKINPAH SITTING ON TOP OF HIS LUGGAGE?

BECAUSE HE WAS ON A CASE!

WHAT DOES JUDGE PECKINPAH KEEP IN HIS POCKET?

JUDGE-MINTS

WHAT IS A GOOD NAME FOR A BIRD LAWYER?

SUE

WHY DO LAWYERS STUDY LAW?

THEY LIKE THE APPEAL!

WHAT SHOULD A LAWYER WEAR TO BIRD COURT?

A LAWSUIT

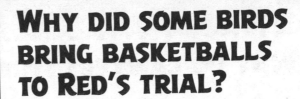

WHY DID SOME BIRDS BRING BASKETBALLS TO RED'S TRIAL?

THEY HEARD THERE WAS A COURT!

WHAT'S THE ONE THING THAT NEVER WORKS WHEN IT'S FIXED?

A JURY

How did Chuck feel about his speeding ticket?

Just fine

Why did the lawyer bring wood to their trial?

In case she needed to make a counter claim

Why were there buckets in the courtroom?

In case someone needed bail

For what did the math teacher get a warning?

An infraction

WHY DID THE POLICE BIRD NAP IN THE BACK ROOM?

IT WAS TIME FOR ARREST!

WHY COULDN'T THE BIRDS COME TO A DECISION?

THE JURY WAS STILL OUT TO LUNCH.

WHY DID JUDGE PECKINPAH BRING A SPARE PAIR OF UNDERWEAR?

YOU CAN NEVER HAVE TOO MANY BRIEFS!

WHY DIDN'T THE DEFENDANT OR THE PLAINTIFF GET A TROPHY?

THERE WAS NO CONTEST.

WHAT DO DEFENDANTS EAT FOR BREAKFAST?

OATH-MEAL

WHY DID JUDGE PECKINPAH GET HIS LUNCH DELIVERED?

HE WANTED ORDER IN THE COURT!

WHY DID TIMOTHY BRING GIFTS TO THE COURTROOM?

HE HEARD THERE WOULD BE MULTIPLE PARTIES!

WHY DID THE COURT REPORTER TURN ON MUSIC?

THEY WERE GOING ON THE RECORD!

WHY WAS JUDGE PECKINPAH'S ARM TIRED?

HE HAD GIVEN A LONG SENTENCE!

WHY DIDN'T MATILDA WEAR JEWELRY TO RED'S TRIAL?

SHE DIDN'T WANT TO BE CHARGED AS AN ACCESSORY!

WHY DID THE OWNER OF THE DRY CLEANER GO TO JAIL?

FOR LAUNDERING MONEY

WHY WAS THE BADMINTON PLAYER ARRESTED?

FOR RACQUET-EERING

It Takes a Village (to Tell a Great Joke)

Bird Village is filled with the best shops and businesses. The birds are always up for a fun and funny day of styling, shopping, and sampling the tastiest treats (especially worms). From haircuts to hugs, these birds can get tickled by anything.

WHAT KIND OF BIRD LIKES TO JOG AROUND TOWN?

A ROADRUNNER

WHAT DO YOU GET IF YOU CROSS A CHICKEN AND A BELL?

AN ALARM CLUCK

HOW DO BIRDS SAY HELLO?

THEY SHAKE WINGS!

WHAT KIND OF BIRDS CAN YOU ALWAYS HEAR COMING?

WHISTLERS

WHY DID RED STOP SHORT?

THERE WAS A STORK IN THE ROAD!

WHAT KIND OF BIRD IS THE OPTOMETRIST?

A SEE-GULL

HOW CAN YOU TELL WHICH END OF A WORM IS WHICH?

TICKLE IT IN THE MIDDLE AND SEE WHICH END LAUGHS!

WHY DO ROOSTERS WORK AT HOTELS?

THEY GIVE EXCELLENT WAKE-UP CALLS.

WHICH BIRD IS THE BEST AT TELLING TIME?

A CUCKOO

WHAT DO WORMS EAT FOR DESSERT?

MUD PIES

WHY WAS THE EARLY BIRD SITTING ON A CLOCK?

HE WANTED TO BE ON TIME!

WHAT'S WORSE THAN FINDING A WORM IN YOUR APPLE?

FINDING HALF OF A WORM IN YOUR APPLE

WHY DIDN'T ANYONE TIP THE HUG TRADER?

THE BIRDS WERE CHEEP!

WHAT DOES RED CALL THE HUG TRADER?

A HUG BUG

DID YOU HEAR ABOUT THE CLIENT WHO WENT TO A RIVAL ACROSS TOWN?

HE WAS A HUG TRAITOR!

WHAT IS THE BEST DAY TO LAY AN EGG?

LAY-BOR DAY

WHAT SHOULD BIRDS READ TO THEIR UNHATCHED EGGS?

A YOLK BOOK

HOW COULD THE NURSE TELL A SET OF NEWBORN TWINS APART?

BY THEIR BIRD-MARKS

HOW DO BIRDS MAKE THEIR HAIRSTYLE EDGIER?

THEY GET FAUX HAWKS!

WHAT KIND OF HAIRCUT MAKES THE MOST NOISE?

BANGS

WHY DID THE STYLIST START WORKING OUT?

HE NEEDED CONDITIONING!

WHY DO BIRDS HAVE THEIR FEATHERS STRAIGHTENED?

TO AVOID FLYAWAYS

WHY DID THE BIRD BRING A PICTURE OF A TREE TO THE SALON?

SHE WANTED HER FEATHERS TO BE STICK STRAIGHT!

WHY DID THE STYLIST TURN UP THE RADIO?

HER CLIENT NEEDED MORE VOLUME.

WHEN DOES A HAIRSTYLE HURT PEOPLE'S FEELINGS?

WHEN IT'S TOO BLUNT

WHY DID THE BIRD BRING A YELLOW MARKER TO HER STYLIST?

SHE WANTED HIGHLIGHTS!

WHAT IS THE FRIENDLIEST HAIRSTYLE?

ONE THAT WAVES

WHY DID THE BIRD SIT ON A LADDER TO GET A HAIRCUT?

SHE WAS INTO HIGH FASHION!

WHAT KIND OF SNACKS DO COLORISTS EAT?

BLONDIES

WHY DID JUDGE PECKINPAH RUN OUT OF THE SALON?

HE WAS SCARED TO DYE!

WHY DID RED ASK THE BARBER FOR DIRECTIONS?

HE WAS GOOD AT SHORTCUTS!

WHY DIDN'T MATILDA LIKE GOING TO THE SALON?

THE STYLIST WOULD ALWAYS TEASE HER FEATHERS!

HOW DID THE BIRD UNRAVEL HER HAIR DRYER CORD?

WITH DETANGLER

WHY DID THE BAKER MAKE A CAKE FOR BOMB'S BIRD-DAY?

IT WAS THE YEAST SHE COULD DO.

WHAT DID THE LOAF OF BREAD SAY TO RED?

"RYE SO SERIOUS?"

WHY WAS THE BAKER'S SON EXCITED?

HE HAD A DATE!

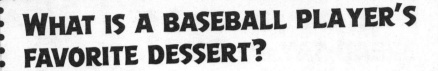

WHAT IS A BASEBALL PLAYER'S FAVORITE DESSERT?

BUNDT CAKE

WHAT KIND OF PIE DOES THE TOWN LOCKSMITH EAT?

KEY LIME

WHY DID THE COOK GO HOME EARLY?

HIS BRAIN WAS FRIED!

WHY DIDN'T STELLA GO TO THE BAKERY?

THE OWNER WAS TOO KNEAD-Y.

HOW CAN YOU GET ONE DESSERT INTO ANOTHER?

USING A FUNNEL CAKE

WHAT DID THE BAKER THINK OF MATILDA'S JOKE?

HE LOAFED OUT LOUD!

WHY DID THE DESSERT HAVE FEATHERS ALL OVER IT?

IT WAS A MOLTEN CHOCOLATE CAKE.

WHAT IS RED'S FAVORITE TYPE OF CUPCAKE?

RED VELVET

WHAT KIND OF TREAT CAN LITTLE BIRDIES NEVER GET ENOUGH OF?

S'MORES

WHAT IS THE MOST HEAVENLY DESSERT?

ANGEL FOOD CAKE

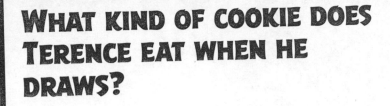

WHAT KIND OF COOKIE DOES TERENCE EAT WHEN HE DRAWS?

SNICKER-DOODLES

WHAT DOES MATILDA LIKE TO SNACK ON?

CHEERY PIE

WHAT KIND OF DESSERT LIKES TO DANCE?

LEMON MERENGUE

WHY WAS SHIRLEY IN A RUSH?

SHE WAS MAKING HASTY PUDDING!

WHY WERE ALL THE SEATS IN THE BAKERY DIRTY?

THE BAKER HAD STICKY BUNS.

WHAT DAY IS THE ICE CREAM PARLOR BUSIEST?

SUNDAE

WHY DID CHUCK ORDER BUTTER PECAN?

HE WAS FEELING NUTTY!

WHAT DID THE SHOP OWNER SAY ABOUT BUSINESS?

IT HAD BEEN A ROCKY ROAD.

95

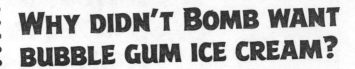

WHY DIDN'T BOMB WANT BUBBLE GUM ICE CREAM?

HE DIDN'T WANT TO BLOW UP!

WHAT FLAVOR DOES THE TOWN BARBER ORDER?

PI-STACHE-IO

WHAT KIND OF ICE CREAM SHOULD YOU BRING TO A PARTY?

CHERRIES JUBILEE

WHY DID TERENCE PUT HIS ICE CREAM IN THE OVEN?

IT WAS COOKIE DOUGH!

WHAT KIND OF ICE CREAM DO THEY EAT AT THE BANK?

MINT CHOCOLATE CHIP

WHAT DID CHUCK ASK THE ICE-CREAM-SHOP SERVER?

"CAN YOU DO ME A FLAVOR?"

BIRDS OF A FEATHER JOKE TOGETHER

Some of the bird's funniest jokes are the ones they tell about themselves. A good comedian is willing to be the punch line, and the birds sure know how to get the last laugh!

WHY DOESN'T CHUCK SHOWER?

HE'D RATHER TAKE A BIRD BATH!

WHY DID MATILDA CALL RED TO CHAT?

SHE WAS FEELING CHIRPY.

WHAT DOES RED LIKE TO CALL HIS HUT?

THE MADHOUSE

WHY DOES MATILDA ALWAYS HAVE CLEAN CLOSETS?

SHE'S AN EXPERT AT HANGER MANAGEMENT!

WHAT DO YOU GET IF YOU CROSS A CHICKEN WITH A SKUNK?

A FOWL SMELL

WHY COULDN'T TERENCE FINISH HIS PAINT YOUR PAIN MASTERPIECE?

HE RAN OUT OF PAIN!

WHY DIDN'T RED WRITE A POEM FOR CLASS?

HE RAN OUT OF RHYME!

WHY DID RED GO TO THE BANK BY HIMSELF?

HE WANTED TO BE LEFT A-LOAN!

WHAT DO YOU GET WHEN YOU CROSS A BIRD WITH A VEGETABLE?

CHICKPEAS

WHY WOULD TERENCE BE A GOOD ENTREPRENEUR?

HE MINDS HIS OWN BUSINESS!

WHAT BRAND OF POWER TOOLS DO BIRDS USE?

BLACK & PECKER

WHERE DOES STELLA SLEEP?

ON A FEATHERBED

WHAT KIND OF BIRD COULD HELP RED BUILD HIS HOUSE?

A CRANE

WHAT IS BOMB'S FAVORITE HOBBY?

PHOTOBOMBING

WHY IS BOMB SO NERVOUS DURING JOB INTERVIEWS?

HE'S AFRAID HE'LL BLOW IT!

WHAT DO YOU CALL THE SMOKE FROM ONE OF BOMB'S EXPLOSIONS?

A BOOM PLUME

WHAT HAPPENED WHEN BOMB EXPLODED AT THE PARTY?

IT BECAME A PARTY FOWL!

WHAT DOES BOMB SAY AT HALLOWEEN?

"WICK-OR-TREAT!"

WHAT IS BOMB'S FAVORITE KIND OF SEAFOOD?

SMOKED OYSTERS

WHAT DID MATILDA THINK OF BOMB'S PARTY?

THAT IT WAS A BLAST

WHY DON'T YOU WANT TO MAKE BOMB MAD?

HE HAS A SHORT FUSE!

WHAT DO YOU GET IF YOU CROSS A HUMMINGBIRD WITH A DOORBELL?

A HUMDINGER

WHAT DID THE YOGA INSTRUCTOR NAME HER EXERCISE PAD?

MATT

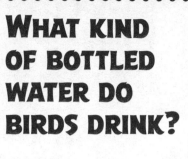

WHAT KIND OF BOTTLED WATER DO BIRDS DRINK?

AVIAN

WHY DOESN'T RED LIKE YOGA?

HE THINKS IT'S FOR POSERS!

WHY COULDN'T THE SQUAB FIND A NEW JOB?

SHE HAD BEEN PIGEONHOLED!

WHAT NOISE DOES BIRD CEREAL MAKE?

SNAP. GRACKLE. POP!

WHAT IS MATILDA'S FAVORITE TV SHOW?

THE HATCHELORETTE

WHICH BIRDS LIKE TO GO ON VACATION?

BIRDS OF PARADISE

WHAT IS A BIRD'S FAVORITE LETTER OF THE ALPHABET?

JAY

WHY DID THE BIRD FROM THE PIZZERIA TRY STAND-UP COMEDY?

HE HAD A GOOD DELIVERY!

WHAT KIND OF BIRD LOVES VEGETABLES?

THE PEACOCK

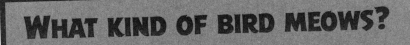

WHAT KIND OF BIRD MEOWS?

THE CATBIRD

What bird stays up past bedtime?

The nighthawk

What birds like to go to concerts?

Rock sparrows

What kind of bird has the most money?

An ostrich

What kind of bird likes to play chess?

The rook

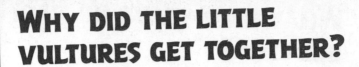

WHY DID THE LITTLE VULTURES GET TOGETHER?

THEY HAD A PREY-DATE!

WHAT DO BUZZARDS DO BEFORE BED?

PREY

WHEN DO HAWKS GET PAID?

PREY-DAY

WHY ARE CLUMSY BIRDS SO WELL-TRAVELED?

THEY ARE ALWAYS GOING ON TRIPS!

WHY DID SHIRLEY GO TO THE LIBRARY?

SHE NEEDED SOME TIME BY HER-SHELF!

WHY DID MIGHTY EAGLE LEARN HOW TO FISH?

HE THOUGHT THE SKILL WOULD COME IN REEL HANDY!

WHAT KIND OF OWL GREW UP ON A FARM?

THE BARN OWL

WHAT KIND OF BIRD LIKES COSTUME PARTIES?

THE MASKED OWL

WHAT KIND OF OWL HAS THE BEST EYESIGHT?

THE SPECTACLED OWL

WHICH OWL SPENDS A LOT OF TIME IN JAIL?

A BARRED OWL

WHAT KIND OF OWL HAS THE BEST HEARING?

THE LONG-EARED OWL

WHAT KIND OF OWL HELPS SANTA CLAUS?

THE ELF OWL

WHY DOES JUDGE PECKINPAH LIKE TO BARBECUE?

HE'S GREAT AT GRILLING!

WHY DOES SHIRLEY LIKE TO VISIT THE CHEESE MAKER?

HE ALWAYS DOES A GRATE JOB!

WHAT SNACK WON'T THE BIRDS EAT NEAR THEIR EGGS?

CRACKERS

WHICH BIRDS ATE THE MOST AT THE PARTY?

THE SWALLOWS

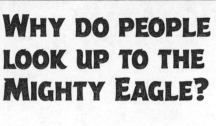

WHY DO PEOPLE LOOK UP TO THE MIGHTY EAGLE?

THEY HAVE TO. . . . HE LIVES ON A MOUNTAINTOP!

WHY IS MIGHTY EAGLE GOOD AT GOLF?

HE ALWAYS GETS A BIRDIE!

HOW WOULD THE MIGHTY EAGLE TRAVEL THROUGH TIME?

THROUGH A WORMHOLE

WHAT DO YOU CALL A BIRD CHEF WHO WAITS TILL THE LAST MINUTE?

A PRESSURE COOKER

WHY WOULDN'T BOMB EAT THE COCONUT CAKE?

HE HAS A NUT ALLERGY!

WHY DID RED, CHUCK, AND BOMB SEEK OUT THE MIGHTY EAGLE?

THEY HOPED HE WOULD TAKE THEM UNDER HIS WING!

WHY DOES EVERYONE LOOK UP TO MIGHTY EAGLE?

HE IS A BIRD OF MANY TALONS.

WHAT IS MIGHTY EAGLE'S FAVORITE SANDWICH?

A HERO, OF COURSE

GO PIG OR GO HOME

All pigs are funny, but some pigs are funnier than others—just ask Leonard, their spokesperson. Even though the pigs are relatively new to Bird Island, they've really embraced the birds' love of a good joke.

HOW DOES LEONARD WRITE TOP SECRET MESSAGES?

WITH INVISIBLE OINK

WHY DID LEONARD MAKE HIS CREW EXERCISE?

THEY NEEDED TO BE IN SHIP-SHAPE!

WHY DID LEONARD HAVE TO HAVE EVERYTHING HIS WAY?

HE WAS PIGHEADED!

HOW DID ROSS KNOW THE BANQUET WAS READY?

A BUZZARD WENT OFF!

WHY DID THE PIG SEND BACK HIS MEAL?

IT WASN'T SLOPPY ENOUGH.

HOW DID LEONARD STEAL THE EGGS?

HE HAD A CRATE IDEA.

WHAT HAPPENED TO THE PIG CHEF WHO BURNED HIS BREAD DURING A COOK-OFF?

HE WAS TOAST!

WHY CAN'T YOU TRUST A PIG WITH YOUR SECRETS?

BECAUSE THEY ALWAYS SQUEAL!

WHY DID IT TAKE THE PIG HOURS TO CROSS THE ROAD?

BECAUSE HE WAS A SLOW-PORK!

How did Red see through Leonard's plans?

They were baloney!

How do elder pigs express disapproval?

"Tusk, tusk."

Who keeps the piggies from jumping too high?

Tram-police

What does Leonard use to eat eggs?

A spork

HOW DO PIGLETS GET FROM HERE TO THERE?

PIGGYBACK RIDES

WHERE DO PIGS GO ON VACATION?

NEW PORK CITY

HOW DO MOST PIG FAIRY TALES BEGIN?

ONCE UPON A SWINE . . .

WHAT IS A PIG'S FAVORITE SONG?

"TWIST AND SNOUT"

WHY ISN'T LEONARD GOOD AT SPORTS?

HE'S A BALL HOG!

WHERE DO PIGS LIKE TO NAP?

IN THEIR HAMMOCKS

WHERE DOES ROSS KEEP HIS MONEY?

IN A PIGGY BANK

WHERE DO PIGS INVEST?

THE LIVESTOCK MARKET

WHAT'S LEONARD'S FAVORITE GAME SHOW?

SQUEAL OF FORTUNE

WHAT PART OF PIGGY ISLAND GOVERNMENT TAKES CARE OF PUBLIC SPACES?

PORKS AND RECREATION

WHAT TYPE OF CANDY DO PIGS ADORE?

LOLLI-PORKS

WHAT HAPPENED TO THE PIG WITH SWINE FLU?

HE WAS SICK, BUT THEN HE WAS "CURED."

WHY DIDN'T THE PIGGIES LIKE THEIR NEW TEACHER?

HE WAS A BOAR.

WHAT IS A PIG'S FAVORITE BALLET?

SWINE LAKE

WHAT IS A PIG'S FAVORITE PLAY?

HAMLET

WHY DID THE PIG DROP OUT OF THE RUNNING RACE?

HE PULLED A HAMSTRING.

WHAT DO PIGS USE WHEN THEY SKIN THEIR KNEES?

OINK-MENT

WHAT'S ROSS'S FAVORITE COLOR?

MAHOGANY

WHAT DO YOU CALL A LUMBERJACK PIG?

A HOG LOGGER

WHAT IS LEONARD'S BEST KARATE MOVE?

THE PORK CHOP

WHY DID THE PIG SPREAD A BLANKET ON THE GROUND?

SHE WANTED TO HAVE A PIG-NIC.

WHAT ARE THE PIGS' FAVORITE PETS?

HAMSTERS

WHO ARE LITTLE PIGS SCARED OF?

FRANKEN-SWINE AND HAM-PIRES

WHAT DO YOU CALL PIGGY BATH TIME?

HOGWASH

HOW DID THE PIG GET TO THE HOSPITAL?

IN A HAM-BULANCE

WHERE DO PIGS PARK THEIR CARS?

THE PORK-ING LOT

WHAT DID ONE PIG SAY TO THE OTHER PIG?

"LET'S BE PEN PALS."

WHY DO PIGS AVOID TOADS?

THEY DON'T WANT TO BECOME WARTHOGS!

WHAT DOES LEONARD SAY TO HIMSELF IN THE MIRROR?

"YOU ARE ONE HAM-SOME PIG."

WHAT DO YOU GET WHEN YOU CROSS A PIG AND A TREE?

A PORKY-PINE

WHAT IS ROSS'S FAVORITE FAIRY TALE?

"PIG-NOCCHIO"

WHAT DO PIGLETS DO AFTER SCHOOL?

HAM-WORK

WHY DO PIGS LOVE MYSTERIES?

THEY LIKE TWISTS IN THEIR TAILS.

WHAT DO YOU CALL A BUNCH OF PIGGIES AT BEDTIME?

PIGS IN A BLANKET

WHAT HAPPENED TO THE PIG WHO LOST HIS VOICE?

HE BECAME DISGRUNTLED.

DID YOU HEAR ABOUT ROSS'S NEW HOME?

IT'S VERY STYLISH.

WHAT DO YOU CALL A BUNCH OF PIGS PLAYING TUG-OF-WAR?

PULLED PORK

WHY COULDN'T THE PIG LACE UP HIS SKATES?

HE WAS TOO HAM-FISTED.

WHAT DO PIGS DRINK AT HOLIDAY TIME?

HOG-NOG

WHAT DO PIGLETS PLAY IN THE SCHOOL YARD?

HOG-SCOTCH

WHAT DO YOU CALL SCHOOL DANCES ON PIGGY ISLAND?

SLOP HOPS

WHAT DO YOU GIVE A PIGLET ON HIS FIRST BIRTHDAY?

A TEDDY BOAR

WHAT'S THE HIGHEST COMPLIMENT YOU COULD GIVE LEONARD?

"YOU'VE MADE A PIG OF YOURSELF."

WHAT KIND OF CAR DOES A FARMER PIG DRIVE?

A PIG-UP TRUCK

WHAT DO YOU CALL A PIG WHO'S CONFUSED?

MISTAKEN BACON

WHAT DO PIGS TAKE WHEN THEY HAVE AN INFECTION?

PIG-ICILLIN

WHAT DO POLITE PIGS SAY?

"BACON YOUR PARDON?"

WHAT DO YOU CALL A SMART PIG?

A REAL EIN-SWINE

WHY DID THE PIG QUIT HIS JOB?

HE FELT HE WAS BEING TAKEN FOR GRUNT-ED.

WHO IS THE PIGS' FAVORITE SUPERHERO?

THE OINK-REDIBLE HULK